My Story Friend

by Kalli Dakos

illustrated by Dream Chen

Magination Press · Washington, DC · American Psychological Association

To my beautiful daughter, Alicia, who always listens
to stories with a loving heart, and to all my story
friends (you know who you are), who have blessed
my life with this precious kind of love—*KD*

To Jun, so happy to become a story friend with you
since 6 years old—*DC*

Books for Kids From the
American Psychological Association

Magination Press is a registered trademark of the American Psychological
Association. Order books at maginationpress.org, or call 1-800-374-2721.

Book design by Rachel Ross
Printed by Phoenix Color, Hagerstown, MD

Library of Congress Cataloging-in-Publication Data
Names: Dakos, Kalli, author. | Chen, Dream, illustrator.
Title: My story friend/by Kalli Dakos ; illustrated by Dream Chen.
Description: Washington, DC: Magination Press, 2021. | "American Psychological Association."
| Summary: "After a long journey, a child finds someone in this world who will listen to their
stories, even the scary ones"–Provided by publisher.
Identifiers: LCCN 2020037797 (print) | LCCN 2020037798 (ebook) | ISBN 9781433836886
(hardcover) | ISBN 9781433836893 (ebook)
Subjects: CYAC: Compassion–Fiction. | Listening–Fiction. | Self-acceptance–Fiction.
Classification: LCC PZ7.D15223 My 2021 (print) | LCC PZ7.D15223 (ebook) | DDC [E]–dc23
LC record available at https://lccn.loc.gov/2020037797
LC ebook record available at https://lccn.loc.gov/2020037798

Manufactured in the United States of America
10 9 8 7 6 5 4 3 2 1

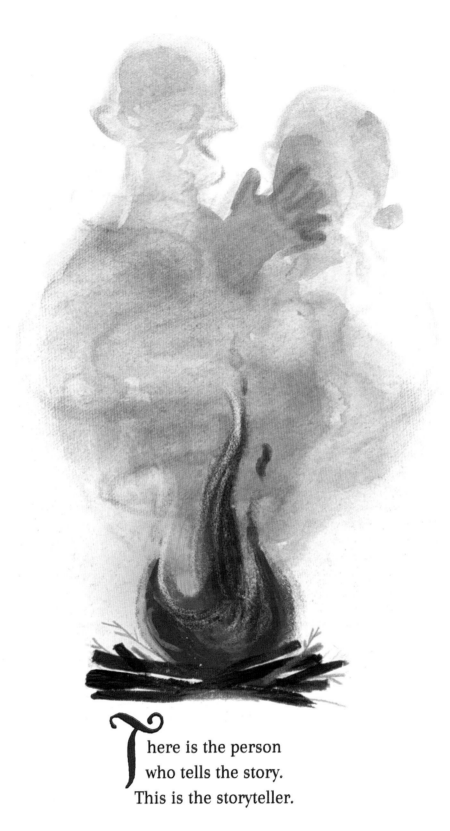

There is the person
who tells the story.
This is the storyteller.

And there is the person
who listens to the story.
This is the story friend.

When I was a child,
my own story
made me very sad.
I knew I had to tell someone
or I might be unhappy forever.

I trekked for miles
across the desert
and into the high hills
where I met the
gruff mountain man
who sells wood in
our village.

"You look brave and strong,"
I said.
"Will you listen to my story?
It is dark and gloomy,
and I might cry when I tell it."

"No," said the mountain man.
"I don't like
tears and sad stories."

I hiked down the mountain,

into a lush green valley,

where I met the farmer
who sells cabbage
at our market.

"Will you listen to my story?" I asked her.
"It is like a dark cloud,
and I might cry when I tell it."

"I'm too busy," she said.
"All these cabbages
have to be shipped to the market
and sad stories upset me."

I journeyed to a wide river,
where the old woman
who tells stories in our village
was toasting marshmallows
on a fire beside
a small house.

I sat down, and she handed me
a stick with marshmallows on it,
and when the heat made them all black,
I said,

"My story is dark,
like these marshmallows.
Everyone is too busy or too afraid to hear it,
and I might cry if I tell it. But if I don't
I will be sad forever."

She looked right into my eyes, and said,
"I will listen to your story."

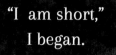
"I am short,"
I began.

"My grandfather
is short.

My grandmother
is short.

My father is short.

My mother is short.

Everyone in my
family is short.

The sad part is
that friends
laugh at me
and call me names.

The really sad part is
that I don't like
my short legs
and my short arms,
and that means,

I don't like ME!

I can't tell
my mother or my father
or anyone in my family
because they don't mind
being short.

But, I do."

Then I put my face in my hands,
and I started to cry.

The old woman
was quiet for a long time,
but when I looked up again
she was crying too,
and our tears
dripped down
and sizzled on the
fire together.

Then she said,
"Sometimes it takes
all the courage
in the world
to tell your story."

"Yes," I cried,
"but what am I
going to do?"

We talked all afternoon,
and I learned
that when we tell our stories
over and over again
to someone who listens
with a big heart,

then our stories become softer
like butter melting in the sun,
and if we are really lucky,
the story tells us what to do.

"I know my great grandfather
won a medal in the war,
and he was probably
the shortest man who fought.

My grandmother is a dairy farmer,
and she provides milk for thousands of people in our land.

And when I look at my mother and father
I see funny and happy and good and kind,
and the best parents in the world
and I could never tell them
how sad I am to be short like them."

"You come from a long line
of brave and good people,"
the woman said.

I sat and thought
and poked at the fire,
and sat and thought
some more.

"I will stop listening
to my friends,
and to my own mind
that tells me short is bad,"
I decided.
"I will listen
to my great grandfather,
my grandmother,
and my parents.

Short can be like them—
brave and strong and kind."

The old woman smiled
when I said these words,
and when it was time to go,
she gave me a big hug.

I journeyed from the river

into the lush green valley,

through the high hills,

and across the desert
back to my home.

I never forgot
where the old woman
lived on the river,
and many times I made
the long journey
to tell her about my life,
and she told me her
stories too.

One day I said,
"You have never been afraid of my stories—
even the dark, stormy ones.

You are
my story friend."

"We can do many things in this world," she replied,
"but listening to each other's stories
is the most precious of all."

The sad day came
when I went to visit
the old woman,
and she was not there.

Someone else was living
in her house.

I will never forget her,
and I will always remember
to tell my own stories,
and to listen carefully
when others
tell me their stories.

We can all be
story friends.

Kalli Dakos is a children's poet and educator. She visits schools across the United States and Canada to encourage children and teachers to write about their own lives. She has written many collections of school poems that include six ILA/CBC Children's Choice selections, such as *If You're Not Here, Please Raise Your Hand.* She lives in Ottawa, Canada, and has an office in Ogdensburg, NY.
Visit kallidakos.com

Dream Chen received her BFA in animation at Communication University of China and her MFA in visual art at the Minneapolis College of Art and Design. She is from China.
Visit dreamchen.org
☐☐ @dreamchenillustration
☐ @dream77225656

Magination Press is the children's book imprint of the American Psychological Association. Through APA's publications, the association shares with the world mental health expertise and psychological knowledge. Magination Press books reach young readers and their parents and caregivers to make navigating life's challenges a little easier. It's the combined power of psychology and literature that makes a Magination Press book special.
Visit maginationpress.org
☐☐☐☐ @MaginationPress